# DISNEY
## PRINCESS

# The
# Princess
# Collection

## Narinder Dhami

PUFFIN

PUFFIN BOOKS

Published by the Penguin Group
Penguin Books Ltd, 80 Strand, London WC2R 0RL, England
Penguin Group (USA), Inc., 375 Hudson Street, New York, New York 10014, USA
Penguin Books Australia Ltd, 250 Camberwell Road, Camberwell, Victoria 3124, Australia
Penguin Books Canada Ltd, 10 Alcorn Avenue, Toronto, Ontario, Canada M4V 3B2
Penguin Books India (P) Ltd, 11 Community Centre, Panchsheel Park, New Delhi – 110 017, India
Penguin Group (NZ), cnr Airborne and Rosedale Roads, Albany, Auckland 1310, New Zealand
Penguin Books (South Africa) (Pty) Ltd, 24 Sturdee Avenue, Rosebank 2196, South Africa

Penguin Books Ltd, Registered Offices: 80 Strand, London WC2R 0RL, England

www.penguin.com

*Cinderella* and *Sleeping Beauty* first published in Puffin Books 2003
*Beauty and the Beast* and *Snow White* first published in Puffin Books 2004
This collection first published 2004
1

Written by Narinder Dhami
Set in 16/19 Perpetua

Made and printed in China by Midas Printing International Ltd

British Library Cataloguing in Publication Data
A CIP catalogue record for this book is available from the British Library

ISBN 0-141-38140-X

# Contents

# Snow White

THE QUEEN PAUSED in front of the golden mirror which hung upon the wall. She was very beautiful, tall and slender, but her face was proud and her heart was as cold as ice.

'Slave in the mirror,' she commanded, 'I summon thee.'

Flames blazed across the mirror and a mask-like face appeared.

The Queen smiled. 'Magic Mirror on the wall,' she began, 'who is the fairest of them all?'

Every day the Queen asked the Magic Mirror the same question, and every day the mirror answered, 'You are the fairest of them all.'

There was silence for a moment.

'Famed is thy beauty, Majesty,' the mirror said softly, 'but a lovely maid I see. Rags cannot hide her gentle grace. Alas, she is more beautiful than thee!'

The Queen turned pale with anger. 'Reveal her name,' she spat furiously.

The mask in the mirror stared back at her. 'Lips red as a rose, hair black as ebony, skin white as snow.'

'Snow White!' the Queen hissed, her face twisted with hatred.

Snow White was the Queen's stepdaughter. The Queen was bitterly jealous of her because Snow White was so beautiful, and, although Snow White was a princess, her stepmother forced her to dress in rags and work as a maid around the castle.

At this very moment Snow White was in the castle gardens on her knees, scrubbing the wide stone steps. Although the Queen made her work hard, Snow White never complained. As she went to draw fresh water from the well, white pigeons fluttered around her, cooing softly.

'Do you want to know a secret?' she asked them. 'Promise not to tell? We're standing by a wishing well. Make a wish into the well, that's all you have to do,' she sang in a sweet voice. 'And if you hear an echo, your wish will soon come true.'

Snow White leaned forwards. 'I'm wishing,' she sang.

I'm wishing . . . came the echo.

'For the one I love, to find me,' she sang.

To find me . . . the echo whispered back.

'Today,' Snow White sang.

'Today!' added a much louder and deeper voice right next to her.

Snow White spun round. A handsome young man was standing at the well beside her. He was richly dressed, looking very much like a handsome Prince in a storybook.

'Oh!' gasped Snow White, feeling very flustered.

'Did I frighten you?' asked the Prince.

Snow White didn't know what to say, so she simply ran off as fast as she could, leaving the Prince staring after her. 'Wait!' he called.

Snow White ran into the castle. She ran up the stairs to the nearest balcony.

She blushed when she saw the Prince was standing below her, singing to her. But Snow White and the Prince were too busy staring at each other to notice the Queen watching them from another window. Her eyes were cold and filled with hatred.

$\mathscr{T}$HE QUEEN SMILED at the huntsman in front of her. 'Take Snow White into the forest,' she said softly. 'Find her some secluded glade where she can pick wild flowers.'

The huntsman nodded, looking a little puzzled.

'And there,' the Queen went on, a cruel smile playing around her lips, 'you will kill her and bring back her heart in this.'

Miserably the huntsman took the carved red box she offered him, knowing he had to do exactly what the Queen said, or his own life would not be spared . . .

Snow White was feeling happy. Her stepmother had allowed her to wear a pretty dress and go for a walk in the woods. One of the royal huntsmen had come to look after her.

Snow White sang softly to herself as she picked an armful of wild flowers. She wondered if she would see the handsome Prince again. Suddenly she spotted a baby bluebird sitting on a rock, chirping sadly.

Snow White knelt down and picked the bird up gently. 'Where's your mama and papa?' she asked. Looking up, she saw them in a tree above. 'There they are. Can you fly?' She held up her hands and released the bird into the air. It fluttered away. The huntsman moved silently towards Snow White. His shadow fell across her and she glanced

up to see his knife. She screamed as the huntsman raised his hand to strike, but then let it drop. He was shaking.

'I can't do it,' he muttered brokenly, and fell to his knees. 'I beg of Your Highness, forgive me.'

'I don't understand,' Snow White cried.

'She's mad,' gulped the huntsman. 'Jealous of you. She'll stop at nothing.' Snow White looked puzzled. 'But – but – who?'

'The Queen,' the huntsman told her. 'Now run. And never come back!'

Snow White ran off as fast as she could, deeper and deeper into the wood. Exhausted and sobbing, she collapsed and buried her face in her arms.

As the darkness lifted, all the animals of the forest stood staring at the sobbing girl lying on the ground. There were deer with their fawns, birds in the trees, and chipmunks, squirrels, racoons, turtles and rabbits.

One brave bunny hopped forward. Snow White lifted her head and gasped.

Startled, the rabbit dived into a hollow log. All the other animals whisked out of sight, too.

'Please don't run away,' Snow White said softly.

The animals began to peer out again.

'Maybe you know somewhere I can stay,' she asked her new friends.

The animals suddenly got very excited, and the birds began to chirp loudly.

'You do?' Snow White exclaimed.

Some of the birds took hold of Snow White's cloak and pulled her after them. Laughing, Snow White followed, along with all the other animals. They walked a little way until they came to a little house. Snow White peered through the window.

'Oh, it's dark inside,' she said, as she knocked at the door. They all waited, but nobody came.

She pushed open the door. 'Hello!' she called politely. 'May I come in?'

No answer. Snow White went in, beckoning

the animals to follow her. 'Why, there are seven little chairs!' she exclaimed. 'There must be seven little children. And, from the look of this table, seven untidy little children.'

'I know!' she said happily. 'We'll clean the house and surprise them. Then maybe they'll let me stay.' She picked up a broom and began to sing. 'Just whistle while you work . . .'

All of the animals were busy. The turtle carried the dirty plates to the sink. The deer dusted the chairs with her tail and the racoons washed all the dirty clothes.

As she swept, she wondered where the seven children were and when they would come home.

*D*EEP UNDER THE ground there was a mine. Seven dwarfs were busily digging for diamonds.

At exactly five o'clock, one of the dwarfs called, 'Hi-ho!'

The other dwarfs immediately stopped digging, shouldered their pickaxes and started to march out of the mine in a long line.

'Hi-ho! Hi-ho! It's home from work we go!' they sang.

As they marched towards their little house, they had no idea what was waiting there for them . . .

Back at the house, Snow White and her animal friends had cleaned everything until it shone. Feeling a little tired, Snow White went upstairs and found a bedroom with seven beds, with a name carved at the bottom of each one.

'Doc, Happy, Sneezy, Dopey –' Snow White laughed. 'What funny names for children. Grumpy, Bashful and Sleepy.'

She yawned and stretched out over three of the beds. Soon she fell asleep.

'Hi-ho! Hi-ho!'

The deer and the fawn were the first to wake up when they heard the noise. In a panic, all the animals dashed for the door and fled to the woods to hide. But Snow White slept on.

'Look!' Doc gasped in horror. 'Our house! The lit's light – the light's lit!'

'Jiminy Cricket!' they chorused. 'Door's open – chimney's smokin' – somethin's in there!'

'Maybe a ghost,' said Happy.

'Or a goblin,' Bashful added.

'Mark my words,' Grumpy said very grumpily. 'There's trouble a-brewin'. Felt it coming all day.'

The dwarfs crept over to the house and tiptoed silently inside. Dopey was last, and slammed the door behind him.

The other six dwarfs glared at him, and put their fingers to their lips.

Doc looked shocked. 'Why! The whole place is clean!'

'Flowers!' said Bashful, grabbing a handful and lifting them out of a vase that was sitting on the table.

He thrust the flowers under Sneezy's nose.

'Don't do it!' Sneezy groaned, staggering back. 'By dose – by hay fever!'

Immediately the other dwarfs rushed over to Sneezy and stuck their fingers under his nose. They only let him go when they had tied up his nose inside his beard.

'Quiet!' Grumpy snapped. 'Do you want to get us all killed?'

Above the dwarfs' heads the bluebirds winked at each other. Then they began tapping on the wooden rafters with their beaks.

'Wha – what's that?' asked Happy, looking scared.

'Sounds close,' muttered Bashful.

The birds started shrieking loudly. Terrified, the dwarfs dived for cover.

'It's up there,' Doc said fearfully.

'Yes, in the bedroom,' Bashful added.

'One of us has got to go down and chase it up,' Doc said bravely. 'Er – go

up and chase it down.'

The other dwarfs all looked at Dopey, who started to sneak away.

'Don't be afraid,' Doc said. 'We're right behind you.'

Dopey gulped. He trailed up the stairs towards the bedroom, and pushed the door open.

At first he couldn't see or hear anything. But then – what was that moving around under the blanket?

With a scream of terror, Dopey turned, ran out of the door and dashed down the stairs.

$\mathcal{A}$LL THE DWARFS gathered around the bedroom door, carrying sticks of wood. As they sneaked inside, Snow White suddenly moaned in her sleep. The dwarfs shrank back.

'Gosh!' the dwarfs whispered. 'What a monster! Covers three beds!'

They gripped their weapons as Doc bravely pulled the blanket away.

'What is it?' asked Happy.

'Why, it's a girl!' replied Doc.

'She's purty,' said Sneezy, staring at Snow White.

'She's beautiful,' sighed Bashful. 'Just like an angel.'

Suddenly Snow White began to stir again.

'She's waking up!' whispered Happy.

'Hide!' Doc ordered.

The dwarfs dashed to hide at the foot of the bed as Snow White sat up and yawned.

The dwarfs peered shyly over the end of the bed.

With a scream, Snow White sat up, pulling the covers around her. Then she looked at the dwarfs more closely. 'Why, you're little men! How do you do?'

The dwarfs looked puzzled.

'How do you do what?' Grumpy snapped.

'Oh, you can talk!' Snow White exclaimed. 'I'm so glad. Now don't tell me who you are, let me guess. I know . . .' she turned to Doc. 'You're Doc!'

Doc nodded and beamed.

Snow White turned to the next dwarf, who was turning red. 'And you're Bashful.'

Sleepy was stretching and yawning. Snow White laughed. 'You're Sleepy.'

'How'd you guess?' asked Sleepy, and the other dwarfs chuckled.

'And you . . .' Snow White moved on to the next dwarf, who was just about to sneeze. 'You're Sneezy.'

Happy began to laugh. 'And you must be –'

'Happy,' interrupted Happy. 'That's me.' He pointed at Dopey. 'And this is Dopey. He don't talk none.'

She looked at the next dwarf in line. 'Ooh, you must be Grumpy.'

Grumpy did not reply.

'Yes,' said Doc, poking Grumpy in the ribs.

Grumpy glared at Doc. 'We know who we are,' he whispered crossly. 'Ask her who she is and what she's doin' here.'

Doc looked serious. He turned to Snow White. 'What are you, and who are you doin' – uh, who are you, my dear?'

'Oh, how silly of me!' said Snow White. 'I'm Snow White.'

The dwarfs looked amazed. 'The Princess?' they said together.

'Yes. Please don't send me away,' Snow White pleaded, her face pale and worried. 'If you do, she'll kill me.'

'Kill you!' the dwarfs repeated. 'Who will?'

'My stepmother, the Queen,' Snow White told them.

'The Queen!' the dwarfs gasped, looking very frightened.

S HE'S WICKED,' Bashful said.

'She's an old witch!' Grumpy said, staring round at the other dwarfs. 'If the Queen finds her here, she'll sweep down and wreak her vengeance on us!'

'But she doesn't know where I am,' Snow White explained.

'She knows everything,' Grumpy warned. 'She's full of black magic.'

'Oh, she'll never find me here,' said Snow White quickly. 'And if you let me stay, I'll keep house for you. I'll wash and sew and sweep and cook —'

'Cook!' the dwarfs repeated eagerly. 'Hooray, she stays!'

Suddenly Snow White remembered the soup she had left cooking on the fire. Jumping out of bed, she ran downstairs to the pot, which was boiling away. She took a spoon and tasted the soup.

'Supper's not quite ready,' she said. 'You'll just have time to wash.'

The dwarfs looked very puzzled.

'Wash!' they said.

Grumpy threw down his spoon. 'Heh!' he said, with a disgusted look. 'I know'd there'd be a catch to it!'

'Let me see your hands. Goodness me,' Snow White said sternly. 'March straight outside and wash, or you'll not get a bite to eat.'

Doc led the dwarfs outside to the tub. 'Don't be nervous.'

Happy stuck his finger in the water. 'Gosh, it's wet!' he said nervously.

'Brr, it's cold too!' said Sneezy, doing the same.

The dwarfs gathered round the tub and began to lather up the soap to wash their faces. Grumpy watched in disgust.

Doc turned and beckoned to the others. Whistling, the dwarfs walked over and surrounded Grumpy.

'Get 'im!' Doc shouted.

The dwarfs immediately pounced on Grumpy and began to scrub him all over with the soap. Grumpy struggled and yelled and grumbled, but he couldn't get away.

Suddenly they heard Snow White calling from inside the house. 'Supper!'

'Food – hooray!' the other dwarfs yelled eagerly. They let go of Grumpy and he fell right into the tub.

*A* SINGLE LIGHT HIGH up in one of the castle windows shone brightly through the darkness. Inside, the Queen stood before the magic mirror, holding the carved red box. She had a very satisfied smile on her face.

'Magic mirror on the wall,' she began softly, 'who now is the fairest of them all?'

Through the flickering flames, the face in the mirror spoke once again.

'Over the seven jewelled hills,
Beyond the seventh fall,
In the cottage of the seven dwarfs
Dwells Snow White,
Fairest one of all.'

The Queen held out the box. 'Snow White lies dead in the forest,' she said, her dark eyes glittering. 'The huntsman has brought me proof . . .' She opened the lid of the box. 'Behold her heart!'

'Snow White still lives, the fairest in the land,' the face said solemnly. ''Tis the heart of a pig you hold in your hand.'

Her face twisted with fury, the Queen gazed down at the box. 'The heart of a pig,' she repeated. 'Then I've been tricked!'

Down, down, down the winding staircase she

went, to the dungeon at the very bottom of the castle. There was a laboratory full of glass jars and tubes and bottles holding purple and blue and black liquids, and shelves of old books. A raven was perched on a skull, fast asleep. He woke with a start as the Queen slammed the door shut behind her.

'The heart of a pig,' she repeated, her voice trembling with rage. She threw the box across the room. 'The blundering fool!'

The raven watched her intently with his bright dark eyes.

'I'll go myself,' the Queen muttered. 'To the dwarfs' cottage with a disguise so complete, no one will ever suspect.'

The Queen reached for one of the books and began to make a formula to transform her beauty into ugliness.

A loud clap of thunder echoed around the laboratory, then died away. The potion was ready. The Queen put the glass of dark green liquid to her lips.

'Now begin thy magic spell,' she murmured, and drank.

Immediately the room began to spin. The glass crashed to the floor as the Queen became dizzy and everything blurred before her eyes.

The Queen began to cackle loudly. 'The perfect disguise!' she announced.

Her beautiful face and tall, slim figure had vanished. Now she was bent and hunched, a wizened old witch. Her hair was white, her nose hooked with a wart on top of it. No one would ever recognize her.

'And now,' the witch's gnarled finger moved down one of the pages of the book, 'a poison apple! One taste and the victim's eyes will close for ever, in the sleeping death!'

The cauldron steamed with a thick green mixture. The witch dipped an apple into the liquid. Pulling it out, the apple slowly turned a deep red.

The witch read from the book again. 'The victim of the sleeping death can be revived only by love's first kiss. Bah!' she muttered. 'No fear of that. The dwarfs will think she's dead. She'll be buried alive!'

The witch placed the ruby red apple on top of her basket and pulled open a trapdoor set into the floor.

'Buried alive!' she chuckled as she climbed through the trapdoor.

*I*T WAS A BRIGHT and sunny morning. As Doc opened the front door, he said, 'Now don't forget, my dear, the old Queen's full of witchcraft. So beware of strangers.'

'Don't worry, I'll be all right.' Snow White lifted Doc's hat and planted a kiss on his head. 'See you tonight.'

Doc blushed. 'Eh – yes, well,' he said, all flustered. 'Come on, men.'

As the dwarfs came out, they all had a warning for Snow White, and she had a kiss for each of them.

'Now I'm warning ya,' Grumpy said sternly, 'don't let nothing or nobody in the house.'

'Oh, Grumpy,' Snow White beamed, 'you do care!' And she bent over to kiss him. Grumpy tried to pull away, but Snow White kissed the top of his head. Muttering, Grumpy marched off, but he couldn't help smiling.

'Goodbye, Grumpy,' called Snow White.

Snow White was singing as she baked seven little gooseberry pies for the dwarfs. The animals were gathered around the window watching her.

'Some day my Prince will come,' Snow White sang happily.

Suddenly, Snow White glanced up to see an ugly old woman standing at the window, smiling at her. Snow White tried not to look frightened, but the old woman was very scary. She had white hair, round staring eyes and a hooked nose with a wart on it.

'All alone, my pet?' the witch chuckled. 'The little men are not here?'

'No, they're not,' said Snow

White politely. She had not forgotten what the dwarfs had said about talking to strangers, but she felt quite safe inside the house. And besides, this was only a poor old pedlar woman.

The witch was sniffing the air. 'Mm, making pies?' she enquired.

'Yes, gooseberry pies,' explained Snow White.

'It's apple pies make the menfolks' mouths water,' the witch said slyly. 'Pies made from apples like these.' She picked the glowing red apple from her basket and held it out to Snow White.

'Oh, they do look delicious,' Snow White agreed.

'Wait till you taste one, dearie!' said the witch with an evil smile.

The birds began to twitter loudly.

The witch thrust her hand through the window. 'Go on. Have a bite.'

Immediately the birds flew down from the trees. They knocked the apple out of the witch's hand, then flew around trying to peck her.

'Oh! Go away,' the witch mumbled, waving her arms. 'Oh, my poor heart! Take me into the house, let me rest. A drink of water – please.'

Snow White helped her in as the animals watched with alarm. They saw the witch smiling to herself as Snow White went for some water. She had the ruby red apple in her hand.

Immediately the animals knew what they had to do. They were going to bring the dwarfs home to save Snow White.

Meanwhile, Snow White had forgotten that she was frightened of the old woman. She

seemed very pleasant and she was offering her a gift . . .

'This is no ordinary apple,' the witch was saying. 'It's a magic wishing apple.'

Snow White's face lit up. 'A wishing apple?' she breathed.

'Yes,' the witch said quickly. 'One bite, and your dreams will come true.'

'Really?' Snow White gasped.

'Yes, girlie.' The witch leaned forward and held out the apple eagerly. 'Now make a wish, and take a bite . . .'

The dwarfs had just arrived at the mine and were collecting their little cart, ready for a hard day's work. But the next moment, Doc cried, 'Look!'

Every animal in the forest was running straight towards them. They began tugging and pulling at the dwarfs' trousers and jackets, trying to hurry them along in the direction of home.

'Go on . . . Git!' Happy shouted.

'The pesky critturs won't stop!' grumbled Doc.

'There's something wrong,' suggested Sneezy.

'Maybe the old Queen's got Snow White,' Sleepy yawned.

The other dwarfs froze.

'The Queen!' Doc gasped.

'Snow White!' The other dwarfs looked at each other in horror.

'The Queen'll kill her!' Grumpy yelled. 'We've got to save her!' He leapt up on to the back of one of the deer. 'Giddy up!' he shouted, and immediately the deer shot away as fast as it could.

The other dwarfs did the
same, and soon all the
animals and the dwarfs
were racing home to
try and save Snow
White. But would
they be too late?

The witch smiled eagerly at
Snow White. 'There must be
something your little heart desires?
Perhaps there's someone you love?' the witch suggested.

Snow White blushed. 'Well,' she said, 'there is someone.'

'I thought so!' She held out the apple. 'Now take the apple, dearie, and
make a wish.'

Snow White gazed at the glowing red apple in her hand. 'I wish . . .' she
began softly.

The witch's evil, staring eyes were fixed on Snow White. 'That's it,' she
urged. 'Go on. Go on.'

The dwarfs and the animals were getting closer and closer now. They were
not far from the little house.

Snow White looked down at the apple. 'I wish that he would carry me
away to his castle, where we would live happily ever after,' she sighed.

'Now take a bite,' the witch said impatiently. 'Don't let the wish
grow cold!'

Slowly, Snow White raised the apple to her mouth and took a bite.

'Oh,' Snow White whispered. 'I feel strange . . .'

Eyes closed, she slid to the floor, and the apple rolled out of her hand.

The witch laughed in triumph. 'Now I'll be the fairest in the land!' Cackling loudly, she hurried out of the cottage. The sky was black now, and heavy rain was falling.

'There she goes!' Grumpy yelled as the deer came galloping towards the little house, all the other animals racing along beside them.

The witch turned, saw the dwarfs and ran for her life. She rushed through the trees, hardly able to see where she was going because of the heavy rain driving in her face.

'After her!' shouted Grumpy.

The dwarfs followed her up a rocky slope that turned into a high ledge and then came to a dead stop. She was trapped.

Suddenly, without warning, a jagged shaft of silver lightning struck the ledge. The rock shattered and, with a scream, the witch fell, all the way down to the ground beneath.

THEIR EYES FULL of tears, the dwarfs were gathered around Snow White. Although she was dead, she still looked so beautiful that the dwarfs could not bear to bury her. So they made a coffin of glass and gold, and kept watch day and night at her side.

Soon everyone was telling the story of the beautiful girl who slept in the forest. The Prince, who had searched far and wide, heard of the maiden in the glass coffin and came to see her for himself. He drew up on his white horse and there in front of him was the scene, just as so many people had described it. The glass and gold coffin with the beautiful, dark-haired girl asleep inside, surrounded by flowers, the seven dwarfs and the animals of the forest keeping watch. The Prince could not believe his eyes. Here was the very same girl he'd fallen in love with in the castle gardens!

The dwarfs watched in wonder as the Prince bent to kiss Snow White and then bowed his head in sorrow.

The victim of the sleeping death can only be revived by love's first kiss . . .

Snow White stirred. Her eyes opened. The dwarfs watched in amazement as the Prince raised his head and saw that Snow White was alive. Smiling, she held out her arms to him, and he lifted her out of the coffin.

The dwarfs hugged each other, and the animals jumped for joy as the Prince carried Snow White gently over to his horse.

'Goodbye!' Snow White said to each of the dwarfs as the Prince lifted them up one by one for a final kiss. 'Goodbye!' she waved.

And then Snow White and her Prince set off for the royal palace, where they would be married and live happily ever after.

# Sleeping Beauty

THERE WAS GREAT excitement throughout the land. At last a baby Princess had been born. King Stefan and his Queen had longed for a child for many years and finally their wish had been granted. Now everyone had gathered to celebrate the arrival of little Princess Aurora.

Inside the castle, the King and Queen were seated on their thrones, smiling proudly at their daughter sleeping peacefully in her cradle.

To a fanfare of trumpets, a herald stepped forward and unrolled a large scroll. 'May I present Their Royal Highnesses King Hubert and Prince Phillip,' he announced loudly.

King Stefan's face lit up. 'Ah, my old friend,' he said, embracing King Hubert.

The two kings were very different – Hubert was as short and round as Stefan was tall and thin – but they had been good friends for many years.

'We have a special gift for your new daughter.' King Hubert beamed. He handed a golden box to his son and gently pushed him towards Aurora's cradle.

Phillip peered in at the baby and pulled a face. King Hubert watched him and smiled at King Stefan. They had already decided that, when Phillip and Aurora were old enough, they would be married. The announcement was to be made this very day . . .

There was another fanfare of trumpets. Everyone turned to look as three glowing sparkles floated into the throne room. Slowly they changed shape, one by one turning into three plump little fairies.

'Their most Honoured Excellencies, the three good fairies,' announced the herald. 'Mistress Flora, Mistress Fauna and Mistress Merryweather.'

The three fairies wore exactly the same long dresses, cloaks and pointed

hats, but Flora's were orange, Fauna's green and Merryweather's blue. Beaming all over their kind, round faces, they flew through the air towards the cradle.

'Oh, the little darling,' Merryweather whispered, peeping in at the baby.

Flora turned to the King and Queen. 'Your Majesties,' she said with a smile, 'each of us the child may bless, with a single gift, no more, no less.' She lifted her wand. 'Little Princess, my gift will be the gift of beauty.' She waved her wand and a shower of flowers fell softly into the cradle.

Then Fauna stepped forward. 'Tiny Princess,' she said, 'my gift will be the gift of song.' With that, sparkling lights drifted down from her wand and into the cradle.

'Sweet Princess,' Merryweather began, 'my gift will be the –'

But the third fairy did not get any further. Suddenly the doors flew open. Everyone gasped as the hall grew dark. Green flames began to flicker up from the floor. Higher and higher they grew, twisting and turning, until they formed themselves into a tall, slender woman dressed in flowing black robes. She wore a horned headdress and carried a slim cane topped with a golden globe. Her presence sent an icy chill through the room.

'Why, it's Maleficent!' Fauna whispered anxiously.

'What does she want here?' Merryweather asked with a frown.

As everyone stood in silence, a large black raven flew in through the open doors. It came to rest on top of Maleficent's cane.

'Well,' Maleficent purred softly, glancing around the throne room, 'quite a glittering party. Everyone seems to be here. Royalty, nobility . . .' Her gaze fell on the three fairies. 'Even the rabble!'

'Ohhh!' Merryweather gasped crossly. She tried to fly at Maleficent, but Flora pulled her back.

'I really felt quite distressed at not receiving an invitation myself,' Maleficent went on silkily.

'You weren't wanted!' snapped Merryweather.

Maleficent put a hand to her throat, pretending to be embarrassed. 'Not wanted!' she cried. 'Oh dear. In that case, I'd best be on my way. And to show that I bear no ill will, I too shall bestow a gift on the child.'

The three fairies gasped in alarm, drawing closer to the cradle.

'Listen well,' Maleficent proclaimed. 'The Princess will indeed grow in grace and beauty, and be beloved of all who know her . . .'

The King took the Queen's hand. They both looked pale and fearful.

'But before the sun sets on her sixteenth birthday,' Maleficent continued, 'she will prick her finger on the spindle of a spinning wheel and DIE!'

Lightning flashed and thunder roared. Seconds later Maleficent was swallowed up in a mass of leaping green flames and she vanished from sight.

'DON'T DESPAIR, YOUR Majesties,' cried Flora. 'Merryweather still has her gift to give.'

The King looked hopeful. 'Then she can undo this curse?'

'Oh no, Sire,' Merryweather replied.

'But she can help,' Fauna added.

Merryweather waved her wand over the baby's cradle. 'Sweet Princess, if through this wicked witch's trick, a spindle should your finger prick, not in death but just in sleep, this fateful prophecy you'll keep. And from this slumber you'll awake, when true love's kiss the spell shall break.'

Merryweather had done the best she could, but the King and Queen were still terrified that Maleficent's evil spell would harm their beloved daughter. So King Stefan ordered that every spinning wheel in the kingdom should be brought to the palace and burnt.

Watching the bonfire, the three fairies knew that would not be enough to stop the evil curse.

'Oh, I'd like to turn that Maleficent into a fat old toad!' Merryweather muttered.

'Now, dear,' said Flora, 'you know our magic doesn't work that way. We can bring only joy and happiness.'

'Well, it would make me happy!' Merryweather replied.

'There must be a way,' Flora went on. Then a smile spread across her face. 'Yes! I believe there is!'

So late that night, the three fairies disguised as peasant women stole out of the castle and into the forest. One of them carried a baby in her arms.

The King and Queen watched sadly from the balcony as Flora, Fauna, Merryweather and Princess Aurora disappeared into the night.

$\mathscr{J}$T'S INCREDIBLE,' cried Maleficent as she stalked around the throne room of her palace on top of the Forbidden Mountain. Her face was pale with fury as she turned on her guards. 'Sixteen years! Sixteen years have passed and not a trace of Princess Aurora anywhere!'

The guards blinked sheepishly.

'She can't have vanished into thin air!' Maleficent snapped. 'Are you sure you've searched everywhere?'

'Yes, everywhere,' mumbled their leader. 'The town, the forest, the mountains. And all the cradles.'

Maleficent turned to face him, her robes swirling around her. 'Cradles? Did you hear that, my pet?' she said softly to her raven. 'All these years, they've been looking for –' she glared at the guards – 'a BABY!'

There was a clap of thunder and the guards shrank back.

'Fools!' Maleficent was furious. She aimed lightning bolts at the guards, who were tumbling down the stairs in their efforts to get away. She turned to the raven. 'You are my last hope. Go and look for a girl of sixteen with hair of sunshine gold.'

The raven flew off through the open window.

'And do not fail me,' Maleficent called after him.

Deep in the heart of the forest was a small woodcutter's cottage. The three fairies had lived here for the past sixteen years, caring for Princess Aurora, whom they had named Briar Rose. They had not dared used any of their magic for fear of Malificent finding her. But today, at last, was her sixteenth birthday and the curse would soon be lifted.

'We'll make a dress,' Flora decided.

'And a cake,' said Fauna.

At that moment, Briar Rose came downstairs. She was tall, slender and beautiful, with long golden hair.

'We want you to go and pick some berries,' said Merryweather, handing Briar Rose a basket.

'I picked berries yesterday,' Briar Rose began.

'We need more, dear,' said Flora quickly. 'But don't go too far.'

'And don't speak to strangers,' Fauna added.

Smiling, Briar Rose went off into the forest. As soon as she had gone, Flora opened a trunk and took out a length of pink material, while Fauna hurried into the kitchen.

'I'll get the wands,' said Merryweather, heading for the stairs.

'No magic!' Flora reminded her. 'I'll make the dress.'

'And I'll make the cake,' said Fauna.

Merryweather stared at them. 'But you can't sew and you've never cooked!'

'This looks awful!' Merryweather complained, staring down at the material wrapped round her.

'That's because it's on you, dear,' Flora retorted.

Fauna slapped some icing and
candles on top of the cake mixture
and stepped back to admire it. 'Well,
what do you think?' she asked.

'Oops!' The icing was sliding on to
the floor. 'It'll be better when it's
baked.'

'I think we've had enough of this nonsense,'
Merryweather said in disgust. 'I'm going to get those
wands!' And she stomped off upstairs.

'Fauna, close all the windows. We can't be too careful, ' said Flora

The three fairies waved their wands. Immediately, the bucket, mop and
broom sprang into action and began to clean the cottage. Flour, eggs and
milk poured themselves into a bowl and began to mix together. Scissors
danced about, cutting the pink material into the shape of a beautiful dress.

Merryweather pulled a face. 'Make it blue!' she insisted, flourishing her
wand.

'No, pink!' Flora argued, waving her own wand.

Blue and pink sparks flew back and forth as the material changed colour
every few seconds. There were so many sparks, some of them flew up the
chimney.

Maleficent's raven was soaring high in the sky overhead. He spotted the
magical sparks whirling out of the chimney straight away and flew down to
take a look.

$\mathcal{B}$RIAR ROSE WALKED through the forest, humming to herself and swinging her basket.

'I wonder, if my heart keeps singing, will my song go winging, to someone who'll find me?' As Briar Rose sang, her voice echoed through the trees, sweet and clear.

Not far away, Prince Phillip was riding through the forest. Like Briar Rose, he was no longer a child. He was now a tall, handsome young man. He pulled his horse up sharply when he heard the faint, sweet sound and smiled.

'You hear that, Samson?' he said, patting the horse. 'Let's go and find out who it is.'

Briar Rose was twirling round on the grass, singing, 'I know you, I walked with you once upon a dream . . .'

Suddenly someone was behind her, gently taking her hands and joining in the song.

Briar Rose spun round. She saw a handsome, finely dressed young man.

'Sorry.' Prince Phillip smiled. 'I didn't mean to frighten you.'

As they stared at each other, both had the strangest feeling that they had met somewhere before.

'What's your name?' Phillip asked.

'It's – it's –' Briar Rose stammered, blushing. 'Oh, I can't!' And she turned and ran.

'But when will I see you again?' Phillip called anxiously.

'This evening.' Briar Rose smiled to herself as she hurried away. 'At the cottage in the glen.'

Briar Rose wandered home in a happy dream, thinking about the handsome man she had just met. Flora, Fauna and Merryweather were waiting for her. The cottage was spotless, the cake looked delicious and the blue dress was beautiful.

'Happy birthday!' the three fairies chorused.

'Oh!' Briar Rose gasped. 'This is the happiest day of my life. Everything's so wonderful.' She smiled at the three fairies. 'Just wait until you meet him!' She began to sing. 'Once upon a dream . . .'

'Him?' Fauna repeated, staring at Briar Rose. 'She's in love!'

'This is terrible!' Flora sighed.

'Why?' Briar Rose looked puzzled.

Fauna took her hands. 'You're already engaged,' she said gently.

'Since the day you were born,' Merryweather added.

'To Prince Phillip, dear,' Fauna explained.

Briar Rose's eyes widened. 'But how could I marry a Prince?' she asked. 'I'd have to be –'

'A Princess,' Merryweather broke in.

'And you are,' Fauna told her. They then told Aurora the whole story.

None of them noticed Maleficent's raven perched near the open door.

'Tonight we're taking you back to your father, King Stefan,' Flora went on. 'And I'm afraid you must never see that young man again.'

Tears welled up in Briar Rose's eyes. 'Oh no!'

Noiselessly, the raven slipped away and flew with haste back to Maleficent's palace.

THE WHOLE KINGDOM was waiting joyfully for the Princess to return home, but no one was more excited than the King and Queen, who hadn't seen their beloved daughter for sixteen years.

'No sign of her yet,' muttered King Stefan, who was staring anxiously out of the window.

'Tonight we toast the future!' Hubert said happily, raising his wine glass. 'Our children will marry and our kingdoms will be united!'

'His Royal Highness, Prince Phillip!' announced a herald, as the young Prince galloped into the castle courtyard on his horse.

'Phillip!' King Hubert jumped to his feet and dashed down the steps to greet his son. 'Hurry, boy. Go and get changed. You can't meet your future bride looking like that!'

'But I have met her, Father,' cried Phillip, laughing.

King Hubert looked amazed. 'You met the Princess Aurora?'

'I said I met the girl I am going to marry,' replied Phillip happily. 'I don't know who she is. A peasant girl, maybe.'

'A peasant girl?' King Hubert gasped in horror. 'No, Phillip, you can't do this to me! You're a Prince and you're going to marry a Princess!'

'You're living in the past, Father,' Phillip said firmly. 'This is the fourteenth century and I'm going to marry the girl I love!' With that, he jumped on Samson's back and galloped off.

Meanwhile, Flora, Fauna and Merryweather were leading Briar Rose across the castle courtyard and into the castle. The three fairies took her to a lavishly decorated bedroom, where a fire had been lit to welcome them.

Flora sat Briar Rose down at the dressing table. 'This one last gift, dear child, for thee,' she said softly, 'the symbol of thy royalty.'

The fairies waved their wands. A gold crown studded with sparkling

jewels appeared and Flora placed it gently on the Princess's head. Briar Rose stared at herself in the mirror and began to cry.

Flora ushered Fauna and Merryweather out of the room. 'Let her have a few moments to herself,' she whispered.

Left alone, Briar Rose sobbed bitterly. She did not notice that the fire was burning brighter, or that wisps of smoke were rising higher and higher into the air.

Briar Rose looked up and saw emerald smoke floating in the air. She stood up as if in a trance. Strange, haunting music played softly as she headed straight for the fireplace.

Outside, the three fairies were talking in low voices. They heard the music drifting out from the room. 'It's Maleficent!'

Pale with terror, the fairies burst into the room. They were just in time to see the brick wall at the back of the fireplace open up and Briar Rose disappear behind it.

In a daze, Briar Rose followed the glowing green smoke up a circular stairway. At the top of the steps stood an open door and she went inside. The wisp of smoke was hovering in the centre of the room. As she walked towards it, it curled and stretched and formed itself into a spinning wheel. At the top of the wheel was a very long, sharp spindle.

'Rose!' Flora, Fauna and Merryweather were hurrying up the stairs. 'Don't touch anything!'

'Touch the spindle!' Maleficent's voice echoed round the room. 'Touch it, I say!'

Briar Rose reached out slowly towards the spindle . . .

THE KING AND Queen were waiting impatiently for their daughter to arrive. The main hall was full of people who had come from all over the kingdom to celebrate. The only person who wasn't happy was King Hubert. He was thinking about how to break the bad news about Phillip to King Stefan.

'Make ready to welcome the Princess!' the herald announced.

Everyone cheered and fireworks began to explode in the dark sky.

In the tower, the Princess was lying on the floor, her golden hair spread around her. She looked pale and still.

The three fairies gently placed her on the bed and now looked tearfully at one another.

'Poor King Stefan and the Queen,' Fauna said softly.

'They'll be heartbroken when they find out,' Merryweather sniffed.

Flora brushed away a tear. 'They're not going to,' she decided. 'We'll put them all to sleep until Rose awakens!'

Quickly, Flora, Fauna and Merryweather flew off around the castle, scattering magic sleep-dust. They began with the guards, who yawned and fell asleep where they stood.

Flora flew over to King Hubert and King Stefan.

'I've – er – just been talking to Phillip,' Hubert said awkwardly, yawning hugely as Flora scattered her sleep-dust, 'and he's fallen in love with some peasant girl …'

But King Stefan was already asleep.

Flora's face lit up. 'A peasant girl!' she gasped, and flew straight over to King Hubert. 'Where did he meet her?'

The King opened one eye. 'Once upon a dream,' he yawned, and then he began to snore.

'Rose! Prince Phillip!' Flora cried excitedly. She hurried back to the others. 'We've got to go to the cottage!'

As they flew out of the castle and returned to the forest, Flora explained what she had discovered – it

was Prince Phillip who Rose had fallen in love with, and he was coming to the cottage tonight. He could save her! But when the fairies reached the cottage, there was no sign of him.

'Look!' Flora had spotted something lying on the floor. She swooped down and picked it up. It was a hat with a feather in it. 'Prince Phillip was here.'

'Maleficent!' Merryweather gasped. 'She's got the Prince!'

'At the Forbidden Mountain,' Flora said, with dread in her voice, but she knew they had to go there.

$\mathcal{M}$ ALEFICENT'S PALACE STOOD, dark and gloomy, on top of the tall, black mountain.

At the bottom of the stairs, in a dark, damp dungeon, sat Prince Phillip, chained to the wall. He looked cold and miserable.

'Oh, come now, Prince Phillip.' Maleficent smiled wickedly. 'Why so sad? In the topmost tower of King Stefan's palace lies the Princess Aurora.' Her smile widened. 'The very same peasant girl you met in the forest! She lies in an ageless sleep. And in one hundred years' time you will be free to leave this dungeon, a grey-haired old man, and ride off to waken your love with love's first kiss!'

Her laughter echoed around the dungeon as Prince Phillip sprang angrily to his feet, straining to break free from his chains.

'A most gratifying day,' Maleficent said with satisfaction as she and the raven left the dungeon.

Wasting no time, the three fairies flew down from the window ledge. Prince Phillip's eyes widened in amazement as they transformed into their normal size.

'Ssh!' Flora tapped the shackles on his arms and they fell away. 'No time to explain!'

Fauna did the same to the chains on his ankles, while Merryweather peeked out of the door, checking for guards.

'Arm thyself with this enchanted shield of virtue and this mighty sword of truth.' Flora waved her wand, and a shield and a sword appeared in the

Prince's hands. 'Now come, we must hurry.'

They all rushed from the dungeon, but only to come face to face with Malificent's raven.

'C AW! CAW!' the raven squawked furiously, and flew back up the stairs to fetch the guards.

Prince Phillip turned and ran the other way, and the fairies bobbed along behind him. They dashed up another staircase as the guards came running towards them. At the top was a window. The fairies flew through it and Prince Phillip jumped after them down into the courtyard. Samson, who was chained too, heard his master and whinnied loudly.

As Merryweather set about burning through Samson's chains with magic, the guards began firing arrows at them. Flora waved her wand and the arrows turned into flowers that simply fell to the ground.

The raven flew up to the throne room to warn Maleficent. Merryweather followed him. The determined little fairy chased him round and round the tower and, with one whisk of her wand, turned him to stone. Then she flew back to join the others.

'Silence!' Maleficent thundered, stalking out of the tower room. 'Tell those fools to –' Her eyes widened as she realized that her raven had been turned to stone. 'NO!'

Now the castle drawbridge was rising higher and higher as Prince Phillip galloped desperately along it.

'Watch out, Phillip!' Fauna cried.

All three fairies waved their wands, helping Samson to make the giant leap from the rising drawbridge to the rocks beyond.

Furiously, Maleficent rushed to the top of the tower and lifted her cane.

'A forest of thorns shall be his tomb,' Maleficent cried, staring at King Stefan's palace in the distance, 'borne through the skies on a fog of doom. Now go with a curse and serve me well. Round Stefan's castle, cast my spell.'

Lightning bolts immediately struck the castle and a great wall of thick thorny branches began to grow, twining upwards to a great height and blocking the Prince's path.

Phillip rode forward, his face determined. He began to hack his way through the thorns. His hands were cut and bruised, but he did not stop until he had forced a way through to the palace.

Maleficent stared in horror. 'No!' she cried, and instantly vanished in a whirl of purple and gold sparks. A second later flames flared in front of Prince Phillip, and Samson reared up in terror as Maleficent appeared.

'Now you shall deal with me, O Prince,' Maleficent hissed, 'and all the powers of HELL!'

The flames leapt higher and Maleficent shot upwards, becoming taller, her shape changing. Seconds later a huge black dragon breathing yellow fire stood in her place.

As the fairies watched, horrified, the dragon spat a stream of flames at Phillip. He fell off his horse and backed away towards the edge of the

cliff. Another blast sent him tumbling over, even closer to the edge. Desperately, he lashed out with his sword at the dragon's head as its long, sharp teeth snapped and snarled. The next blast knocked the shield from the Prince's grasp.

'Ha ha ha!' Maleficent's evil laughter echoed through the flames as the dragon moved in for the kill.

Quickly, the three fairies touched the Prince's sword with fairy dust.

'Now sword of truth, fly swift and sure,' Flora cried, 'that evil die and good endure!'

Prince Phillip pulled back his arm and hurled the sword with every bit of strength he possessed. It buried itself deep in the dragon's chest. With a cry, the wounded creature stumbled forward, then plunged over the edge to the bottom of the cliff.

PRINCE PHILLIP HURRIED through the castle courtyard. He saw people sleeping where they stood as he headed towards the tower room where Aurora lay.

The three fairies watched happily as he bent over the bed and gently kissed her. Her eyes opened slowly and she smiled as she recognized the Prince. There was no need for words.

Throughout the castle, everyone else began to wake up. King Stefan and his Queen opened their eyes. So did King Hubert.

'Now, Hubert, you were saying?' Stefan turned to his friend.

'Well . . .' King Hubert looked embarrassed. 'To come to the point, my son Phillip says he's going to marry –'

There was a blast of trumpets. As everyone turned, Phillip and Aurora came down the stairs smiling, hand in hand.

'It's Aurora!' King Stefan cried in delight. 'She's here!'

King Hubert rubbed his eyes in disbelief as Aurora ran into her mother's arms. Up on the balcony, the three fairies smiled at each other, tears of happiness in their eyes.

'I – I don't understand!' King Hubert stammered.

Aurora smiled and kissed him on the cheek, and then, as the music began, she danced off across the floor with her Prince.

'Oh, I love happy endings!' Fauna sobbed.

'So do I,' Flora agreed. Then she frowned as she noticed Aurora's blue dress. 'Pink!' she whispered, lifting her wand.

'No, blue!' Merryweather replied, changing the dress back again, as the Prince and Aurora danced on, knowing that now they would live happily ever after.

# Cinderella

'WAKE UP, CINDERELLA!'

Cinderella yawned and opened her eyes. She smiled to see two bluebirds perched upon her pillow, singing sweetly.

'Oh,' she sighed, 'I was having such a lovely dream.'

Her face fell as she considered the day that lay ahead of her: cooking, cleaning, washing, ironing, running around after her stepmother, Lady Tremaine, her two stepsisters, Drizella and Anastasia, and their fat, spoilt cat, Lucifer.

And whatever I do, it's never enough, Cinderella thought sadly. They always want me to do more.

Her thoughts flew back to when her father was alive. Then she had been loved and given everything she wanted. But her father had died soon after marrying her stepmother and now Cinderella was nothing more than a slave in the big, beautiful house where she had been brought up. Sometimes she felt that her only friends were the animals who lived in the house and out in the barnyard: the birds, the mice, her old horse and her dog, Bruno, who had been a present from her father when she was a little girl.

Cinderella washed and dressed, singing to herself. Then she hurried down the stairs to the next landing, opening the curtains on her way. She slipped into her stepmother's bedroom, which was still in darkness. Next to the bed was a fat, black cat.

'Lucifer,' Cinderella whispered. 'Come here.'

The cat got grumpily to his feet and stalked out of the door, tail waving.

'It's not my idea to feed you first in the mornings,' Cinderella said, hurrying down the stairs. 'It's Stepmother's orders.' And Cinderella knew what would happen if she didn't do as she was told . . .

'*C*INDERELLA!' CALLED a cross voice. 'Cinderella!'

'All right,' Cinderella sighed. 'I'm coming.'

Quickly, she poured the tea and made up three breakfast trays. She hurried out of the kitchen and up the stairs.

'Good morning, Drizella,' she said cheerfully, pushing open the door of the first bedroom. 'Huh!' Drizella sniffed, and snatched a tray. 'Take that ironing —' she pointed at a basket heaped with crumpled clothes — 'and have it ready in an hour.'

Cinderella picked up the basket and went into the second bedroom.

'Well, it's about time!' Anastasia grumbled. 'Don't forget my mending.'

'Yes, Anastasia,' replied Cinderella, handing her a tray and picking up her basket. Then she went to her stepmother's room.

'Come in, child.' Her stepmother was a tall, thin, elegant woman with a pale, cruel face.

'Good morning, Stepmother,' Cinderella said, handing her a tray.

'Pick up the laundry and get on with your duties,' replied her stepmother coldly.

Cinderella hurried out with the three baskets. As she reached the top of the stairs, she heard a bloodcurdling scream from Anastasia's bedroom.

Anastasia ran out screaming. 'She put it there!' she shrieked, glaring at Cinderella. 'A big ugly mouse! Under my teacup!'

Cinderella looked startled. Why had one of her tiny friends been hiding under the teacup? Then she saw Lucifer looking very smug.

'All right, Lucifer,' Cinderella said as the cat stared innocently at her, 'what happened to the mouse?' She lifted up the cat and a fat little mouse rolled out from under his paws. 'Oh, you poor thing!' Cinderella cried.

Looking terrified, the mouse dashed off and disappeared down a hole.

'Cinderella!' Her stepmother's voice rang out. 'It seems you have time on your hands for playing vicious practical jokes.'

'But –'

'Silence!' Lady Tremaine reached for the teapot. 'But perhaps we can put that time to better use. There are the carpets to be cleaned, and all the windows too. And, oh yes –' she smiled an evil smile – 'the tapestries to be washed.'

'But I just finished –'

'Do them again!' her stepmother thundered. 'Then scrub the terrace and clean the halls. And –' her smile deepened – 'see that Lucifer gets his bath.'

'IT'S HIGH TIME he got married and settled down!'

'Yes, Your Majesty,' the Duke agreed quickly. 'But we must be patient. Maybe if we just left the Prince to find his own wife –'

'No, I have a much better idea!' the King retorted. 'We'll hold a ball here at the palace. And we'll invite all the most eligible ladies in the kingdom.' He laughed. 'Soft lights, romantic music. It can't fail!'

'V-very well, Sire,' the Duke stammered. 'I'll arrange the ball for –'

'Tonight!' the King broke in. 'And see that every girl in the kingdom is there. I'm going to make sure my son finds a wife! Understand?'

Cinderella scrubbed the marble floor. She was tired but was only halfway through cleaning the lower hall. In the distance she could hear her stepmother at the piano as Drizella and Anastasia practised their singing.

There was a knock at the door. Cinderella hurried to open it.

'An urgent message from His Imperial Majesty!' a messenger announced.

'Whatever can this be?' Cinderella thought, staring at the letter as she went over to the music room.

'This came from the palace,' Cinderella explained, holding up the letter.

'The palace!' shrieked Drizella. She rushed across to Cinderella and snatched the letter from her.

'Let me have it!' Anastasia roared, grabbing it from her sister.

'I'll read it.' Cinderella's stepmother took the letter and opened it. 'Well!' A satisfied smile spread across her thin face. 'There is to be a ball, in honour of the Prince! And every girl in the kingdom is to attend.'

Cinderella clasped her hands in delight. 'That means I can go too!'

Drizella burst into mocking laughter. 'Her dancing with the Prince! Ha ha!'

'It says every girl in the kingdom,' Cinderella pointed out.

Her stepmother glanced at the letter. 'So it does,' she said silkily. 'I see no reason why you can't go, if you get all your work done. And if you can find something suitable to wear.'

'I'm sure I can,' Cinderella agreed happily. 'Thank you, Stepmother!' And she ran lightly from the room.

'Mother!' Drizella moaned. 'Do you realize what you just said?'

'Of course,' her mother replied, with a wry smile. 'I said *if*.'

CINDERELLA WHIRLED ROUND the room, holding a dress against her, as the birds and the mice watched. 'It was my mother's. It is a little old-fashioned, but I'll fix that.'

Humming happily, Cinderella fetched her sewing basket.

'Cinderella!'

Cinderella sighed. 'Oh, now what do they want? My dress will just have to wait,' she said, hurrying over to the door.

For the rest of the day Cinderella didn't have a minute to herself. Her stepmother kept finding jobs for her to do. She ran up and down the stairs a hundred times, ironing dresses, tying ribbons and cleaning shoes. With a heavy heart, she realized that she wasn't going to have time to prepare her own dress. She wouldn't be able to go to the ball.

As night began to fall, Cinderella watched the carriage arrive.

'You're not ready, child,' said her stepmother, sneeringly.

'I'm not going,' Cinderella replied sadly.

A hint of a smile played around her stepmother's lips. 'Not going? Oh, what a shame.'

Trying not to cry, Cinderella rushed to her room. She gazed out of the window at the brightly lit palace in the distance.

Suddenly light flooded her room. Cinderella gasped as she turned to see a beautiful dress before her. It was her dress, and it looked wonderful. The sleeves had been shortened, the collar had been changed, it had a new sash and it had been trimmed with ribbons and beads.

Cinderella couldn't believe her eyes. 'You did all this?' she said to her little animal friends. 'How can I ever thank you?'

Quickly, she pulled off her rags and slipped into the new dress. It fitted perfectly. She ran down the stairs, catching up with her stepmother and stepsisters in the lower hall as they made their way to the carriage.

They stared in amazement at Cinderella and her beautiful dress. Drizella and Anastasia were furious.

Their mother fingered the beads round Cinderella's neck.

'Why, they're MY beads!' shouted Drizella, pulling them from Cinderella's neck.

'And that's my sash!' shrieked Anastasia, grabbing it and tearing Cinderella's skirt.

They pulled and ripped at her dress until it was ruined.

'Goodnight, Cinderella,' said her stepmother, smiling triumphantly.

S OBBING AS IF her heart would break, Cinderella ran out into the garden. She sank down on to a bench. Now her dreams would never come true...

'My dreams are no use at all,' she sobbed as Bruno, the mice and her other animal friends watched her anxiously. 'There's nothing left to believe in any more.'

Suddenly someone began to stroke her hair. 'You don't really believe that, my dear,' said a kindly voice.

Cinderella looked up. Through her tears she could make out an elderly woman with a smiling face and twinkling blue eyes. Cinderella had never seen her before, but she liked her immediately.

'Oh, but I do mean it!' she gulped.

'Nonsense, child,' said the woman. 'If you meant it, I wouldn't be here. So dry those tears. You can't go to the ball looking like that. Now what did I do with my magic wand?' She began to look around her.

'Magic wand?' Cinderella repeated, wondering if she'd heard correctly. 'Why, then, you must be –'

'Your fairy godmother, of course.' She waved her arms and her wand appeared. 'And the first thing we need is a pumpkin.'

Cinderella's eyes opened wide. 'A pumpkin?'

Her fairy godmother glanced around the garden and picked out a fine, fat pumpkin. She tapped it with her wand and the pumpkin turned instantly into a glittering golden carriage.

Then the fairy godmother looked down at the group of mice watching timidly. With one flash of her wand, they became elegant white horses.

'You can't go to the ball without a coachman,' she went on.

She waved her wand at Cinderella's old horse and he turned into a coachman. Next, she turned Bruno into a smartly dressed footman.

'Well, hop in, my dear.' Cinderella's fairy godmother ushered her towards the coach. 'We can't waste any time.'

'B-but,' Cinderella stammered, 'don't you think my dress –'

Her fairy godmother looked startled at the torn frock. 'Good heavens!' she cried. 'You can't go in that!' She lifted her wand and magic sparks

whirled around Cinderella. Looking down, she saw she was wearing a dazzling blue dress and glass slippers. It was like a dream come true!

Her fairy godmother looked grave. 'But like all dreams, I'm afraid this one can't last forever, my dear. You must be home by midnight. At the stroke of twelve, the spell will be broken and everything will be as it was before!'

$\mathcal{T}$HE CASTLE BALLROOM was filled with people dressed in their finest clothes. Candles cast a soft light as musicians played. The handsome Prince and his father were greeting the girls, one by one.

Looking anxious, the King turned to the Duke. 'He doesn't seem interested in any of them!' he muttered.

At that moment the Prince caught his father's eye and yawned.

'Drizella and Anastasia Tremaine, daughters of Lady Tremaine,' announced the herald.

The Prince looked taken aback as Drizella and Anastasia hurried forward, but he bowed politely.

The King took one look at the sisters and groaned.

At that moment, the Prince spotted Cinderella entering the ballroom. Their eyes

met. Cinderella smiled shyly and immediately the Prince hurried past Drizella and Anastasia towards her and took her hand. Together they began to dance. They had eyes for no one else. Drizella and Anastasia watched furiously.

'Who is she, Mother?' Drizella wailed.

'She certainly seems familiar,' their mother replied thoughtfully.

Cinderella and the Prince danced on. Then they walked in the garden and talked, just the two of them, and Cinderella felt as if she was living in a beautiful dream. As the Prince bent to kiss her, she closed her eyes.

BONG!

'Oh!' Cinderella gasped. 'It's midnight!'

'Yes.' The Prince looked puzzled. 'But –'

'I must go! Goodbye!' And with that, Cinderella picked up her skirts and ran off through the palace.

'But I don't even know your name!' the Prince cried after her.

But Cinderella was hurrying down the castle steps. In her haste, one of her glass slippers loosened and fell off.

With no time to spare, Cinderella left the slipper where it was and jumped into the carriage. The coachman shook the reins and the horses galloped off as the clock continued to chime.

'I'M SORRY, Your Majesty,' the Duke explained nervously, 'but all we could find was this glass slipper.'

The King bounced out of bed, looking furious. 'What! You mean you don't know her name or where she lives?'

The Duke shook his head. 'But the Prince is determined to marry her, Sire,' he went on hastily. He held up the glittering glass slipper. 'He swears that he'll marry none but the girl this slipper fits.'

'He said that, did he?' The King looked pleased. 'This slipper might fit any number of girls in my kingdom. We'll find him a wife yet!' He turned to the Duke. 'Try this slipper on every girl in the land,' he ordered, 'and if the shoe fits, bring her to me!'

Shortly afterwards, the King's messengers were busy going around the city posting notices announcing that every unmarried girl had to try on the glass slipper. The girl it fitted would be the Prince's bride. Everyone was very excited.

Lady Tremaine came across one of the royal proclamations and rushed back home immediately.

'Cinderella!' she called sharply as she took off her cloak in the entrance hall. 'Where are my daughters?'

'I think they're still in bed,' Cinderella replied.

Lady Tremaine brushed past Cinderella and went upstairs to wake up her daughters. 'Hurry now, get up,' she urged.

'Huh?' Anastasia mumbled from under the covers. 'Why?'

'Because the Duke will be here any minute!' her mother replied. 'He's been looking for that girl all night. They say the Prince is madly in love with her!'

Cinderella had been carrying the breakfast tray down the landing. The tray slipped from her hands and the cups and saucers smashed on the floor into a thousand pieces.

ᵉ𝒴OU CLUMSY LITTLE fool!' Lady Tremaine stalked out on to the landing to find Cinderella on her hands and knees picking up broken bits of crockery. 'Clear that up quickly, then help my daughters to dress.'

'What for?' Drizella moaned.

'If he's in love with that other girl, why should we even bother?' Anastasia demanded sulkily.

'Now, listen to me,' said their mother sternly. 'There is still a chance that one of you can marry him. No one, not even the Prince, knows who that girl is. The glass slipper is the only clue.'

Cinderella's heart leapt as she heard that.

'And if one girl can be found whom the slipper fits,' Lady Tremaine went on, 'that girl will be the Prince's bride.'

Drizella and Anastasia looked thrilled.

As Cinderella stood there dreamily holding the tray, the sisters piled heaps of clothes upon it. Cinderella didn't even notice. She was thinking about her handsome Prince.

'Wake up, stupid!' Drizella yelled at Cinderella.

'We've got to get dressed!' Anastasia roared.

'Yes.' Her eyes still dreamy, Cinderella glanced down at herself. 'Oh, yes, we must get dressed,' she agreed.

She pushed the clothes into Drizella's arms and walked off.

'Mother!' Drizella wailed. 'Did you see what she just did?'

'Quiet!' Lady Tremaine watched Cinderella waltzing down the landing. She was humming to herself. It was the same song that she and the Prince had danced to the night before. Was it really possible that the Prince had fallen in love with Cinderella?

Lady Tremaine's eyes narrowed. Now she knew the identity of the mysterious owner of the glass slipper. Quietly, she followed Cinderella along the landing and into her room. The smile on Cinderella's face vanished as she looked up and saw Lady Tremaine whisk the key from the lock and pull the door tightly shut.

Lady Tremaine ignored Cinderella's cries. She slipped the key into her pocket and went back to her daughters. She didn't notice that the mice had seen what she had done. Two of them sneaked downstairs after her, determined to get hold of that key and let Cinderella out.

'Mother!' Anastasia and Drizella were calling excitedly. 'He's here! He's here!'

A golden coach was drawing up outside the house. Inside sat the Duke, holding the glass slipper on a velvet cushion. Drizella and Anastasia immediately rushed over to the mirror and began preening themselves.

'Girls!' Lady Tremaine held up her hand. 'Now remember. This is your last chance. Don't fail me.' She opened the door to the Duke.

'Why, that's my slipper!' Drizella announced loudly as the footman held out the velvet cushion.

Anastasia glared at her. 'Well, I like that!' she snapped. 'It's *my* slipper!'

Anastasia pushed Drizella out of the way and sat down. The footman slid the slipper on to her foot. 'It's exactly my size!' she exclaimed triumphantly, but everyone could see that the slipper was much too small for her.

The Duke pointed at Drizella. 'Now the next young lady.'

Meanwhile, one of the mice was climbing down into Lady Tremaine's pocket, with the other holding fast to his tail. The key was big and heavy, but at last they managed to pull it out. Immediately, they scampered off with it. Huffing and puffing, they hauled the key up the stairs. Cinderella watched them through the keyhole of her room.

But then a shadow fell over the mice. It was Lucifer. Quick as a flash, the cat sprang towards them and trapped one of the mice as well as the key under an upturned bowl.

'Fetch Bruno!' Cinderella called desperately to the other mice.

The dog was snoozing in the sunshine out in the yard. Quickly, the birds flew down and began to pull at his tail and ears, trying to wake him up.

Back inside, Drizella grabbed the glass slipper from the footman, announcing, 'I'll do it myself,' and she crammed her toes in.

Her mother smiled as Drizella held out her foot. 'It fits!' she declared.

But suddenly Drizella's foot burst out of the slipper, which flew up into the air, to be safely caught by the footman.

Meanwhile, Bruno was dashing into the house and up to Cinderella's

room. There he came nose to nose with Lucifer. He growled loudly. He'd been waiting for this day for a long time!

Looking scared, Lucifer backed right up to the window ledge. As Bruno jumped towards him, Lucifer fell backwards and tumbled out of the window.

Downstairs, the Duke and the footman were now ready to leave.

'You are the only ladies of the house?' the Duke asked.

'There's no one else, Your Grace,' Lady Tremaine replied.

'Your Grace!' Cinderella called from the top of the stairs. 'May I try the slipper on, please?'

$\mathcal{D}$RIZELLA AND ANASTASIA looked on in disgust as Cinderella ran lightly down the stairs towards them, a happy smile on her face. The Duke led her over to the chair, and the footman hurried across with the glass slipper.

Lady Tremaine slyly stuck out her cane, right in front of the footman. He gasped as he tripped and fell heavily. The slipper flew from the cushion, hit the floor and smashed into a million tiny slivers.

'Oh, no!' the Duke groaned, as Lady Tremaine smiled smugly. 'This is terrible! What will the King say?'

'But I have the other slipper!' Cinderella said.

She slipped her hand into her apron pocket and pulled out the identical shining slipper. Lady Tremaine was horror-struck, and Drizella and Anastasia were, for once, unable to say a word.

The Duke slid the glass slipper on to Cinderella's slender foot and, needless to say, it fitted perfectly.

So Cinderella and the Prince were married. Everyone in the whole kingdom was invited to join in the celebrations, including Cinderella's friends the mice, the birds and Bruno. Everyone, that is, except her cruel stepmother and stepsisters. And, of course, Lucifer!

# Beauty and the Beast

Once upon a time, a young Prince lived in a shining castle. Although he had everything his heart desired, the Prince was spoiled, selfish and unkind.

When an old beggar woman came to the castle looking for shelter from the bitter cold, the Prince was disgusted by her ugliness and he sneered at the rose she offered him.

But the woman was really a beautiful enchantress. She had seen that there was no love in his heart. As punishment, she transformed him into a hideous beast and placed a spell on the castle and all who lived there.

The rose she had offered was an enchanted rose. She told him that if he could learn to love another and earn her love in return by the time the last petal fell, the spell would be broken. If not, the Prince would be doomed to remain a beast for all time.

$\mathcal{B}$ELLE SKIPPED OUT of the cottage she shared with her father and walked through the village to the bookshop.

'Good morning,' said Belle to the bookseller. 'I've come to return the book I borrowed.'

'Finished already?' asked the bookseller.

'Oh, I couldn't put it down!' she explained. 'Have you got anything new?'

'Not since yesterday!' the bookseller chuckled.

'That's all right,' she said, pulling one off the shelf. 'I'll borrow this one. It's my favourite. Far-off places, magic spells, a Prince in disguise . . .'

Belle wandered down to the fountain in the town square, and sat down to read.

Suddenly a shot rang out from a musket fired by a tall, handsome man.

'Wow, Gaston!' said a short, tubby man admiringly. 'You're the best hunter in the world. No beast alive stands a chance against you. And no girl, for that matter!'

Gaston stuck out his chest like a proud peacock. 'It's true,' he admitted. 'And I've got my sights set on that one.' He pointed his musket at Belle.

Lefou looked surprised. 'The inventor's daughter?'

'She's the one,' Gaston replied. 'The most beautiful girl in the town and the lucky girl I'm going to marry!'

Gaston stepped behind Belle and snatched the book from her hands.

'Belle, it's about time you got your head out of those books and paid attention to more important things. Like me!'

'Maybe some other time,' said Belle quickly. 'I have to get home to help my father.'

Lefou burst out laughing. 'That crazy old loon!'

Gaston laughed, too, and Belle glared at them.

'My father is not crazy,' said Belle crossly. 'He's a genius.'

Suddenly they heard a loud explosion from Belle's cottage. Next moment, smoke began to drift out of the windows.

Belle ran home in a panic. Her father was kicking his latest invention, which was supposed to chop and stack wood.

'I'll never get this bonehead contraption to work!' Maurice sighed.

'Yes, you will,' Belle told him. 'And you'll win first prize at the fair tomorrow.'

Belle rooted in the box of tools and gave one to her father to fix the machine.

After a while, Maurice reached for a lever and pulled. The machine whirred as an axe fell and chopped a piece of wood in half. The wood flew through the air and landed on the pile of logs beside the fire.

'It works!' cried Belle, and she hugged her father as more logs hurtled past. 'You did it! You really did it!'

'I'm off to the fair!' Maurice said proudly.

'Goodbye, Papa! Good luck!'

NIGHT WAS FALLING and Maurice was worried. 'We should be there by now,' he muttered to his horse, Philippe. 'Maybe we missed a turn. Let's go this way.'

Philippe whinnied with alarm and shook his head. The route Maurice wanted to take led through a scary tunnel of tangled trees, into a heavy mist. Maurice coaxed Phillip towards the scary path.

Suddenly a wolf streaked across in front of them. Philippe reared up and Maurice fell to the ground as more wolves howled loudly all around them. Philippe backed away in terror and then fled.

Thunder howled, lightning crashed and it was raining heavily. Maurice ran through the forest as fast as he could, but the wolves were gaining on him. Suddenly, there in front of him was a castle gate!

Maurice fell inside and kicked the gate shut, just as the wolves leapt in for the kill.

The castle looked dark and frightening, but at least he was safe. He pounded on the huge oak doors, which opened, just a crack. Maurice peered inside. The entrance hall was enormous. It was only dimly lit, with a few candles here and there.

Maurice shut the door behind him. 'Hello?' he called nervously. 'Is there anyone there?'

A wooden clock and a silver candlestick stood on the table. As Maurice turned away, the clock spoke to the candlestick in a warning voice. 'Not a word, Lumiere. Not one word.'

'I don't mean to intrude,' Maurice was saying, 'but I need a place to stay.'

Lumiere chuckled. 'Of course, Monsieur,' he called to Maurice. 'You are welcome here.'

Maurice looked round in terror. 'Who said that?'

He grabbed Lumiere and held the candlestick up, so that he could look into all the dark corners.

'Over here!' Lumiere said.

Maurice whirled round in a panic. He couldn't tell where the voice was coming from. Lumiere tapped Maurice on the forehead with one of his candles. Maurice was so shocked he dropped Lumiere on the floor.

Cogsworth, the clock, jumped down. 'Well, you've done it now, Lumiere,' he blustered. 'Splendid! Just peachy.'

'You are soaked to the bone, Monsieur,' Lumiere said kindly. He hopped towards the drawing room. 'Come. Warm yourself by the fire.'

Lumiere led Maurice to an armchair in front of the blazing fire. Maurice sat down as a footstool with a wagging tassel of a tail bounded up to him, barking loudly.

'Would you like a nice spot of tea, sir?' said a sweet-faced teapot, busily pouring tea into a small cup with a tiny chip on the side.

Maurice sipped the tea, and the little cup giggled.

'His moustache tickles, Mama!' Chip said.

Maurice smiled and said hello to the little cup and then . . .

BANG! The door slammed. A cold wind rushed into the room and put out the fire.

A huge snarling beast walked into the room on all fours. He was powerfully built, and covered in fur with horns on his head.

Shaking all over, Maurice turned to look at the Beast.

'Who are you?' the Beast demanded, baring his fangs. 'Why are you here?'

'I was lost in the woods,' Maurice gasped. 'And —'

'You're not welcome here!' the Beast roared, lunging forward.

'Please!' Maurice begged desperately. 'I meant no harm! I just needed a place to stay.'

'I'll give you a place to stay,' the Beast growled, grabbing Maurice's collar in his claws.

'Oh no!' Maurice cried, as the Beast carried him over to the door.

IN FRONT OF Belle's cottage, a wedding party had gathered. There was a red carpet on the grass, and a table laden with food.

Gaston cleared his throat, and addressed the crowd. 'I'd like to thank you all for coming to my wedding.' He smirked. 'First I'd better go in there and propose to the girl!'

Inside, Belle was reading a book when she heard a knock at the door. She got up to answer it.

'Gaston,' said Belle, backing away from him. 'What a pleasant surprise.'

'Isn't it, though?' Gaston boomed. 'This is the day your dreams come true! Picture this. A rustic hunting lodge. My latest kill roasting on the fire.' He kicked off his boots. 'My little wife massaging my feet while the little ones play on the floor with the dogs. And you know who that little wife will be?' Gaston smirked. He jumped up and trapped her against the door. 'You, Belle!'

Belle gasped. 'I'm very sorry,

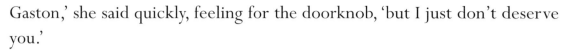

Gaston,' she said quickly, feeling for the doorknob, 'but I just don't deserve you.'

She opened the door just as Gaston tried to kiss her, and he tumbled outside. There was a loud splash, and Gaston ended up head first in the duck pond.

Gaston stood up. 'I'll have Belle for my wife,' he snarled. 'Make no mistake about that!'

Later, Belle peered out. 'Can you imagine,' Belle said crossly to a little hen, 'Me – the wife of that brainless . . .'

Suddenly Philippe came racing out of the forest. Belle knew something was wrong. 'Where's Papa?' she cried. 'You have to take me to him!'

Philippe had brought Belle to the castle. She was nervous but she was determined to find her father. She opened the big oak doors and began to walk up the stairs. Cogsworth and Lumiere watched her climb staircase after staircase until she reached the top of the tower.

'Is anyone here?' called Belle, pausing at the top of the stairs.
'Belle?'

With a cry of joy, Belle ran across the dark, musty chamber and knelt down to take her father's outstretched hand through the bars of his cell.

'Who's done this to you?' Belle demanded angrily.

Maurice looked around in a panic. 'No time to explain! You must go!'

'I won't leave you!' cried Belle.

At that moment, a claw gripped Belle's shoulder.

She gasped as she was pulled away from the door.

'What are you doing here?' roared a furious voice.

'Who are you?' Belle asked, her voice trembling.

'The master of this castle,' growled the Beast.

'I've come for my father,' Belle said bravely. 'Please let him out. He's sick!'

'He's my prisoner,' the Beast snarled.

'Take me instead,' cried Belle bravely.

The Beast scowled. 'You? You would take his place?'

'If I did, would you let him go?' Belle asked in a determined voice.

'Yes,' the Beast agreed. 'But you must promise to stay here forever.' The Beast stepped out of the shadows into the dim light. Belle gasped in horror when she saw his face.

'No, Belle!' Maurice grabbed his daughter's shoulder through the bars. 'I won't let you do this.'

'You have my word,' Belle told the Beast.

The Beast released Maurice and dragged him down the stairs, ignoring all his pleas. A coach without horses stood at the gate.

'Take him to the village,' ordered the Beast and the coach immediately trundled away.

Lighting their way with Lumiere's flames, the Beast led Belle to a much pleasanter part of the castle. Tears trickled down Belle's cheeks. Lumiere whispered in his master's ear. 'Say something to her!'

The Beast looked puzzled at this suggestion. Awkwardly, he growled, 'The castle is your home now, so you can go anywhere you like. Except the west wing.'

'What's in the west –?' Belle began.

The Beast whirled round in a fury. 'It is forbidden!' he roared.

The Beast flung open the door of one of the rooms. 'Now, if you need anything,' he growled, 'my servants will attend you.'

'Invite her to dinner!' whispered Lumiere.

'You will join me for dinner!' the Beast thundered. 'That's not a request!'

He slammed the door shut behind Belle. Running over to the bed, she sank down on her knees, and burst into tears.

'ᗯHO DOES SHE think she is?' Gaston grumbled. 'That girl has tangled with the wrong man!'

It was snowing outside, but the village tavern was snug and warm. Gaston and Lefou were drinking beer with some of the townsfolk.

Suddenly the doors burst open and Maurice staggered in. 'Someone help me!' he cried. 'He's got her locked in a dungeon!'

'Who?' asked a man.

'Belle!' Maurice replied, 'We must go. Not a minute to lose!'

Gaston leaned forwards in his chair. 'Whoa! Slow down, Maurice,' he said calmly. 'Who's got Belle locked in a dungeon?'

Eyes wide with terror, Maurice described the Beast. As he did so some of the customers began to laugh.

'All right, old man,' Gaston said, wickedly. 'We'll help you out.' And with that, two men picked up Maurice and threw him out of the tavern.

'Crazy old Maurice,' said one of the men.

'He's always good for a laugh!' said the other.

'Crazy old Maurice, hmm?' said Gaston thoughtfully. 'I have a plan.' He knew Belle would do anything to protect her father, so he arranged a meeting with the doctor from the town asylum.

In the dining room, the Beast was pacing impatiently up and down, waiting for Belle to come down to dinner.

'Master,' Lumiere began nervously. 'Have you thought that this girl could be the one to break the spell?'

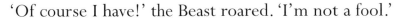

'Of course I have!' the Beast roared. 'I'm not a fool.'

'Good,' said Lumiere. 'So you fall in love with her, she falls in love with you and poof!' he blew out his candles, 'the spell is broken! We'll be human again by midnight.'

'Oh, Lumiere,' scolded Mrs Potts, the teapot. 'These things take time.'

The Beast said despairingly, 'But she's so beautiful, and I'm —' He held out his claw, staring at the sharp talons. 'Well, look at me!'

'Oh, you must help her to see past all that,' said Mrs Potts firmly. 'You can start by trying to act like a gentleman.'

'And you must control your temper!' chorused Lumiere and Mrs Potts.

Cogsworth poked his head into the room.

'Where is she?' the Beast demanded. When he heard she wasn't coming, he burst out of the room and ran up the grand staircase.

'I thought I told you to come down to dinner!' the Beast thundered, banging on Belle's door.

'I'm not hungry,' called Belle.

'Fine!' the Beast growled. 'Then go ahead and starve!' He glared at Cogsworth and the others. 'If she doesn't eat with me, she doesn't eat at all!' and he stomped off to his room in the west wing. He stared at the wilting

rose, encased in glass. It was dying and along with it his dream of becoming human again. Belle would never see him as anything but a monster.

♡

DOWN IN THE kitchen, Mrs Potts was trying to put her teacups to bed. She stopped suddenly as she saw Belle in the kitchen doorway.

'Splendid to see you out and about!' said Cogsworth, smiling at Belle. 'I am Cogsworth, head of the household, and this is Lumiere. If there's anything we can do to make your stay more comfortable . . .' began Cogsworth.

'Well, I am a little hungry,' admitted Belle.

'Hear that?' Mrs Potts asked excitedly. 'She's hungry!' She turned to the stove. 'Stoke the fire! Break out the silver.'

The stove turned his burners on and knives, forks and spoons stood upright.

'Remember what the master said,' Cogsworth snapped.

'Oh pish tosh!' sniffed Mrs Potts, looking down her nose at Cogsworth. 'I'm not about to let the poor child go hungry.'

Lumiere led Belle over to the dining room, and opened the door.

Trollies laden with covered plates immediately rolled into the room from the kitchen. The plates leapt on to the table and settled in front of Belle. She watched in amazement as every dining-room object came to life, singing and dancing, offering food of every description. She took a

taste of everything as it went by.

Belle laughed and clapped her hands.

'It's my first time in an enchanted castle –'

'Enchanted!' Cogsworth interrupted her. 'Who said anything about the castle being enchanted?'

'I figured it out for myself!' Belle laughed. 'I'd like to look around, if that's all right.'

Cogsworth reluctantly began a tour. He took her to a long hallway lined with suits of armour. But Belle was more interested in the tall, dark staircase leading to the west wing.

'What is he hiding up there?' she asked.

'Hiding?' Lumiere stammered. 'The master is hiding nothing.'

'Then it wouldn't be forbidden,' Belle replied, and took a step forward.

Cogsworth and Lumiere jumped to block her path.

'Perhaps Mademoiselle would like to see the library?' Cogsworth suggested.

Belle looked interested. 'You have a library?'

'With mountains of books!' Lumiere beamed at Belle.

As he and Cogsworth set off arm in arm for the library, Belle ran quietly up the stairs.

At the end of a long, dark corridor was a room. Inside, broken furniture lay on the floor, and there was a ripped portrait of a handsome Prince.

As Belle stared curiously at the picture, a glowing pink light caught her eye. It came from a rose underneath a glass cover. Belle walked over to the table, and lifted off the glass case. But as she reached out to take the flower, the Beast leapt into the room from the balcony. He snarled viciously, grabbing the case and replacing it gently over the rose.

'I warned you never to come here!' he growled.

'I didn't mean any harm!' gasped Belle.

The Beast smashed a corner of the table. 'Get out!' he bellowed.

Belle turned and ran for the door. 'Promise or no promise,' Belle panted, her eyes wide with fear, 'I can't stay here another minute!'

A moment later, Belle was on her way home, clinging tightly to Philippe's back. The horse had been waiting patiently outside.

As Philippe trotted through the snowdrifts, four sinister shadows were lurking among the trees. Belle and Philippe heard snarling and growling, and four wolves slunk out of the undergrowth straight towards them. Philippe kicked out desperately with his hoofs. One wolf managed to jump on to the horse's back. Another wolf leapt towards Belle.

THE BEAST HURLED the wolf away. The other wolves attacked. They jumped on the Beast, sinking their teeth into him. Roaring, the Beast lashed out, hurling the wolves right and left. Realizing they were defeated, the wolf pack fled.

Covered in blood, the Beast collapsed to the ground. Belle helped the Beast on to Philippe's back.

When they got back to the castle, Belle dabbed the Beast's wounds with a cloth. The Beast roared with pain. 'That hurts!'

'If you'd hold still, it wouldn't hurt as much!' Belle replied sharply. 'By the way,' she added shyly, 'thank you for saving my life.'

The Beast looked surprised. 'You're welcome,' he muttered.

As the days went on, Belle felt less afraid of the Beast. They did more and more things together and Belle came to see that there was goodness in him.

'Tonight is the night!' said Lumiere to the Beast as he was getting ready for dinner. 'When the moment is right, you must confess your love . . .'

The Beast hung his head. 'I can't do it.'

'You care for the girl, don't you?' asked Lumiere.

'More than anything,' the Beast grunted.

'Then you must tell her,' Lumiere advised.

Cogsworth appeared in the doorway. 'Your lady awaits,' he announced.

Belle looked more beautiful than she had ever looked before. The Beast greeted her looking smart and groomed. They smiled at each other and, arm in arm, they walked down to dinner. Afterwards, they danced in the ballroom. It was a perfect night and the sky was full of stars. Belle sat down

on the balcony, and nervously the Beast moved closer to her.

'Belle –' he began, remembering what Lumiere had said. 'Are you happy here with me?'

'Yes,' replied Belle, but she admitted that she so missed her father.

The beast led Belle up to the west wing and picked up a magic mirror.

'This mirror will show you anything,' he told her.

Belle took the mirror eagerly. 'I'd like to see my father,' she said.

The mirror glowed and there was her father struggling against the storm towards the castle to find Belle. As she watched, he collapsed on to the ground and lay there, motionless.

Belle gasped in horror. 'Oh, no! He's sick!' Clutching the mirror, she stared up at the Beast. 'He may be dying, and he's all alone.'

The Beast looked down at the drooping rose. Sadly he said, 'Then you must go to him. I release you.'

'You mean I'm free?' Belle asked, shocked.

'Yes,' the Beast replied.

Belle stared into the mirror again. 'Hold on, Papa,' she cried. 'I'm on my way.'

BELLE FOUND MAURICE lying in the snow. She took him home and watched over him as he lay sleeping on his bed. Suddenly his eyelids fluttered open.

'Belle!' he croaked. 'How did you escape?'

'I didn't escape, Papa,' replied Belle. 'He let me go.'

Maurice shook his head in disbelief. 'That horrible beast?'

'But he's different now, Papa,' said Belle, eagerly. 'He's changed.'

Suddenly the satchel Belle had brought with her from the castle moved and tipped over. The magic mirror fell out, along with Chip.

Belle and her father laughed. 'A stowaway!'

There was a rap at the door. Standing there was the doctor from the asylum saying he'd come for her father.

Belle was shocked. 'My father's not crazy!' she shouted.

'He was raving like a lunatic!' yelled Lefou. Gaston, who was lurking in the shadows, smirked.

'Maurice!' called Lefou gleefully. 'Tell us again, old man, just how big was this beast?'

'He was enormous! Eight, ten feet!' Maurice exclaimed.

'Well, you don't get much crazier than that!' Lefou announced.

The doctor signalled to his attendants to grab Maurice.

Gaston stepped forward. 'I might be able to clear up this little misunderstanding. If . . .'

'If what?' asked Belle eagerly.

'If you marry me,' Gaston smirked.

'Never!' she cried, furiously. 'I can prove my father's not crazy!' She ran to get the magic mirror. 'Show me the Beast!' she commanded.

The mirror glowed and the Beast appeared, roaring savagely.

'Is he dangerous?' called one of the townswomen in a frightened voice.

'Oh no!' Belle replied. 'No, he'd never hurt anyone. I know he looks vicious, but he's really kind and gentle . . .'

Furiously Gaston tore the mirror from Belle's grasp. 'She's as crazy as the old man!' he yelled, showing the townsfolk the mirror. 'The Beast will make off with your children. He'll come after them in the night!'

The crowd shouted in agreement. 'Kill him!'

To stop them running off to warn the Beast, Gaston locked Maurice and Belle in the cellar. Then he led the townsfolk towards the castle.

COGSWORTH, LUMIERE and Mrs Potts saw the angry mob crossing the bridge.

'Quick! Warn the master!' Cogsworth ordered. 'If it's a fight they want, we'll be ready for them!'

A parade of furniture marched down the stairs. The chests of drawers, cupboards, lamps and chairs were all ready to fight. Outside, the mob rammed the door with a battering ram until it swung open. Gaston peered round suspiciously. But all he could see was furniture.

Beckoning to the crowd, Gaston led them towards the stairs. Lumiere, who was standing very still on a table, was grabbed by Lefou.

'NOW!' Lumiere shouted and all the furniture sprang to life, attacking the townsfolk. The coat rack punched, a mop knocked people down. The carpet rolled up one person and the others were hit with frying pans and spoons and cauldrons.

Seeing that the townsfolk were losing the battle, Gaston hurried away and sneaked up the staircase to find the Beast . . .

Chip was desperately trying to think of a way to help Belle and Maurice. Suddenly he noticed Maurice's firewood-chopping machine. Steaming and chopping wildly, the machine began rolling across the yard. The axe chopped right through the cellars doors, and the machine crashed down into the cellar. Belle and Maurice were free.

At the castle, the battle was still in full swing. Soon the townsfolk began fleeing for their lives. The furniture cheered triumphantly.

In the west wing, Gaston stepped into the Beast's room, his bow and arrow at the ready.

The Beast saw him but he did not move. With Belle gone he didn't want to live. Gaston let fly with the arrow, and hit the Beast in the shoulder. He roared out in pain.

Gaston charged forward, pushing the Beast through the windows on to the balcony. He fell heavily, very close to the edge.

'What's the matter, Beast?' Gaston asked mockingly. 'Too kind and gentle to fight back?'

The Beast's head drooped. He still did not move, not even when Gaston raised a club over his head.

Lightning flashed. Philippe came galloping across the bridge with Belle and Maurice clinging to his back. Belle glanced up and saw the Beast and Gaston on the roof.

'No!' Belle screamed.

The Beast looked down. 'Belle!' The very sight of her gave him hope and strength. He fought back until he had Gaston by the throat, dangling over the edge of the roof.

'*L*ET ME GO! Please!' Gaston begged in a terrified voice. 'Don't hurt me! I'll do anything!'

The Beast stared at him. The anger faded from his face. He pulled Gaston back on to the roof and set him safely down.

'Get out,' the Beast said, giving him a shove.

Belle ran out on to the balcony above them.

'Belle.' The Beast smiled up at her. 'You came back.'

Suddenly he was roaring in pain. Gaston had stabbed the Beast in the back.

Belle watched in horror as Gaston raised the knife to strike the final blow. But as he did so, he lost his balance. The knife fell from his hand and, with a shout of terror, Gaston toppled backwards off the roof, to his death.

Belle pulled the Beast up on to the balcony. Mrs Potts, Lumiere and Cogsworth dashed into the room, and gasped when they saw how badly injured their master was.

Belle laid the Beast's head gently on the floor, and stroked his cheek. 'We're together now. Everything's going to be fine, you'll see.'

The Beast stroked her face. 'At least I got to see you . . . one last time.'

He closed his eyes and his head fell back.

'No! No!' Belle sobbed. 'Please, don't leave me! I love you . . .'

The last petal fell from the enchanted rose.

Suddenly, magical sparks began to shower down on to the balcony. A cloud of smoke wrapped itself around the Beast like a cloak as his paws

became human hands and his face became the face of a handsome Prince.

When the Prince awoke, he stared down at himself in wonder, then turned to Belle.

They kissed. The spell had been broken.

'We're human again!' cried Lumiere, Cogsworth and Mrs Potts.

The footstool, now a dog again, ran in barking. He had a small boy, Chip, riding on his back.

The Prince and Belle laughed, and gazed at one another happily.

'Are they going to live happily ever after, Mama?' Chip asked.

'Of course, my dear,' chuckled Mrs Potts. 'Of course!'

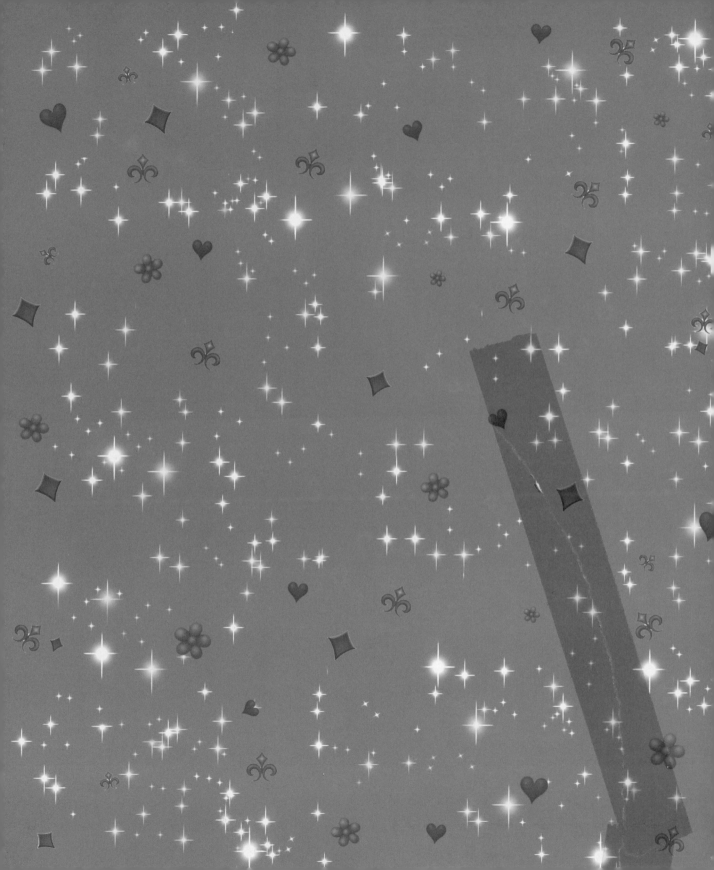